Breathe

Wildmark Publishing

Paperback ISBN: 978-1-7398245-5-6
Hardcover ISBN: 978-1-7398245-6-3

Text by Becky Hemsley
Illustrations by Siski Kalla

Cover design and typesetting by Ryan Webb

First Edition, 2022

Breathe

Becky Hemsley & Siski Kalla

She sat at the back
    and they said she was shy,
She led from the front
    and they hated her pride,

They asked her advice
and then questioned her guidance,
They branded her loud,
then were shocked by her silence,

When she shared no ambition they said it was sad,
So she told them her dreams and they said she was mad,
They told her they'd listen, then covered their ears,
And gave her a hug while they laughed at her fears,

And she listened to all of it
thinking she should,
Be the girl they told her to
be best as she could,

But one day she asked
     what was best for herself,
Instead of trying
     to please everyone else,

So she walked to the forest
        and stood with the trees,
She heard the wind whisper
        and dance with the leaves,

She spoke to the willow,
  the elm and the pine,
And she told them what she'd
  been told time after time,

She told them she felt she was never enough,
She was either too little or far far too much,

Too loud or too quiet,
    too fierce or too weak,
Too wise or too foolish,
    too bold or too meek,

Then she found a small clearing surrounded by firs,
And she stopped...and she heard what the trees said to her,

And she sat there for hours
not wanting to leave,

For the forest said nothing,
it just let her breathe.

Where do you like to BREATHE?

There are many special places that can make you feel calm and peaceful. Some places are small and cozy, while others are wide open and airy. Some places aren't exactly places at all, but more about who you're with or what you're doing. You are the only person who can say which place makes you feel best. Don't see your special place here? Draw it or describe it! How does it look, what is the sound like, and why do you think it makes you feel calm?

Are there people or animals who help you feel calm?

Do you find some activities calming? Cooking, drawing, playing an instrument, perhaps?

Do you like to spin, to dance, or to put headphones on and listen to sounds that make you feel good?

Do you have a special toy or blanket that helps you feel calm?

Lots of people find green or blue spaces in nature especially calming. Planting and growing flowers, herbs and other plants is wonderful too.

Small spaces or home-made hidey holes can feel especially cozy and safe.

And, of course, books are a wonderful way to feel calm, and to BREATHE!

Author

Becky loves taking a walk in nature - through the forest, along the beach or in the snow. It reminds her to take a moment to breathe. Autumn is her favourite season because it gives her an excuse to wear big sweaters and drink lots of hot chocolate! She is happiest when spending time with her family and loves reading bedtime stories to her children.

She is the author of *Talking to the Wild: the bedtime stories we didn't know we needed*, and *What the Wild Replied*, published by Wildmark Publishing

Illustrator

Painting watercolours — especially of trees, flowers, children and animals — makes Siski calm and happy, as does swimming in or just looking at water. She also loves swinging in a hammock, and eating scones with jam outside on a summery afternoon. More than anything, Siski loves children's books. She would eat them if she could. But they don't taste as good as scones.